No Bones About It:

A DOG LOVER'S INSPIRATIONAL POEMS

JILL MEUNIER

No Bones About It:

A DOG LOVER'S INSPIRATIONAL POEMS

(2ND EDITION)

ReadersMagnet, LLC

No Bones About It: A Dog Lover's Inspirational Poems (2nd Edition)
Copyright © 2022 by Jill Meunier

Published in the United States of America
ISBN Paperback: 978-1-955603-93-5
ISBN eBook: 978-1-955603-92-8

All rights reserved. No part of this publication may be reproduced, stored in a retrieval system or transmitted in any way by any means, electronic, mechanical, photocopy, recording or otherwise without the prior permission of the author except as provided by USA copyright law.

The opinions expressed by the author are not necessarily those of ReadersMagnet, LLC.

ReadersMagnet, LLC
10620 Treena Street, Suite 230 | San Diego, California, 92131 USA
1.619.354.2643 | www.readersmagnet.com

Book design copyright © 2022 by ReadersMagnet, LLC. All rights reserved.
Cover design by Ericka Obando
Interior design by Mary Mae Romero

Contents

Introduction 8

Weenie's Story 10

A Wish Upon a Dog 14

Old Dog 16

Love Triangle 18

She's A Mess 20

Vices Versus 22

Table for One 24

My Body, My Dog 26

You Can't Get Over Me 28

I Fed Your Dog Tonight 30

New Puppy 32

So Together 34

View from a Gucci Bag 36

The Daily Bark 38

Hard as a Nail 40

Perfect Fit 42

$$ Rich vs. Poor $$	44
Drug Dog	46
I Just Want to BE	48
Just another Walk in the Neighborhood	50
Belly Up	52
Faith, Hope and Charity	54
Puppy UP	56
I'm Waiting	58
Pocket Dog	60
Reincarnation	62
A Dog, A Sack, And A Phone	64
Stayin' Home	66
She Shows Me	68
The Small Print	70
A Doggie Day	72
I Hate Rain	74
My Favorite Eats	76
Dog-Free Zone	78
Twenty Minutes	80
Gypsy	82

Dear Neighbor..................................84

2 Gray Hairs....................................86

Double Doggie Grief............................88

Separation Anxiety.............................90

He Doesn't Care 92

My Eyes 94

I'm Lost 96

I am a High Desert Dog.........................98

First Christmas 100

The Measure of a Smile 102

The Farewell Dog 104

I, Dog, Will Never Leave 106

Not Too Late 108

Introduction

I love dogs. Need I say more? No, but I will.

I didn't have a dog as a pet until my young adult years when everyone and everything else on earth seemed to have let me down. I was a rebellious, rowdy, eccentric girl childwho still managed to make the honor roll. I was repeatedly told by my mother that I was a good-for-nothing nut-case, and suffered a childhood and young to mid-life adulthood of constant verbal violence and severely abusive critique. This treatment left me very insecure and with a lifetime of chronic and clinical depression and anxiety.

Until I met DOGS.

Like the zillions of other people on the planet who love dogs for all the right reasons, ALL dogs became my quintessential best friends and family. Their lives and love superseded the length and quality of most other relationships of my life. As repayment for them bestowing themselves on my world, I will glorify them in making THE DOG the one who is serving up his near-human thoughts in most of my poems – the rest being a combination of typical canine-ness and humanity, and the emotions evoked between them.

Please enjoy my 2nd book, an inspirational poetic tribute to DOGS, a book for all ages.

Weenie's Story

She was a portrait of disfigured beauty.
A rescue literally dying to come into my world.
A boney puppy girl with an imperfect but gorgeous face, marred by an exxxxtreme overbite.
I scooped up this wonderful she-prize and nursed her back to health, even buying a special flat bowl so that she could eat and lap her food with her shark-like jaws.
This is the photo of her I took after 30 days in our home with a bounty of food and LOVE.
FINALLY SMILING, is all can say about Weenie's recovery – and 14 wonderful years together.
Weenie, departed our lives in April 2011
Always in our hearts.

Lady in a Dog's Life

She may have her daily work
Routine that keeps her busy
She comes home stressed and overwhelmed
And sometimes in a tizzy
She has her hobbies, chores and meals
Exercise, shopping and making deals
Caring for the house and its residents
Unaware she's setting precedents
Hustle and bustle makes her driven
Her obligations keep her livin'
Does she ever stop to breathe?
What else does she have up her sleeve?
She catches herself crying
From time to time unexplained
Amidst her heavy sighing
Her composure not yet reclaimed
You might think I like
The salty tears I lick away
But for me, a devoted dog
It's just another day

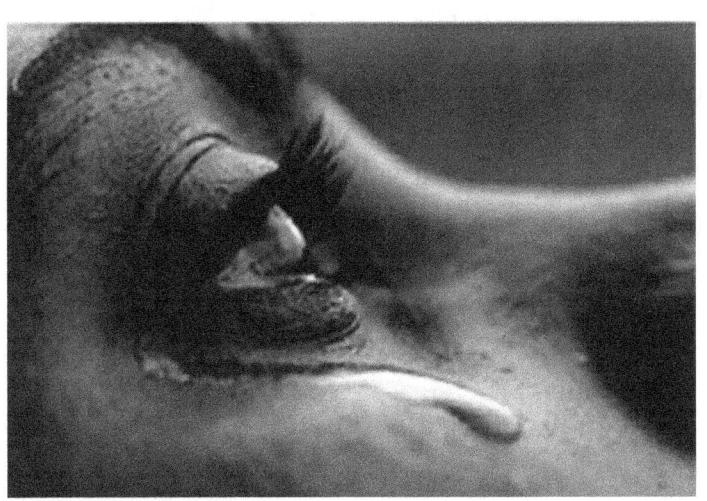

A Wish Upon a Dog

I want a dog
To make my world complete
My landlord says no
But that's not a cause for defeat
I'll just keep trying to push the notion
Way before my heart is broken
Cuz I just cannot afford to move
I'm here for a while and in the groove
Sometimes I feel so very alone
Looking to find that cuddly BONE
A kindly friend will get me through the fog
Cuz I just wanna get a dog

Old Dog

I'm a crusty old dog
And here are just the facts
I'll lay like a log and
Let her hold up the wax
For she's a brand new puppy
Full of vigor and pee
A replacement there can never be
I told the psychic and it was no lie
I didn't want you to see me die
But as the ticking time draws near
Our love envelopes us ever dear
I'm not ready yet but I'll let you know
When I'll float into the doggie bistro
You might return from your to-do spree
For life and death is like it be
You may find me in the kibble café lounge
Just know, I've joined the other hounds
So for now 'til then I'll just take it slow
I've had my time and you've made it glow
Embrace the little one as you did me
Then let my memory set you free

Love Triangle

They were born triplets
A threesome we raved
We helped ease them outward
A loving road we paved
Before these tiny lives drifted
From mother's furry silk
These precious pups were gifted
With the Dog-God's milk
There was so much to go 'round
'T was a hand in a glove
6 Nipples
3 Bellies
ONE LOVE

She's A Mess

She Yacks and barks on phones all day
And complains that her life is wasting away
I feel helpless, full of sorrow
Will she making it "til tomorrow
I can't help wondering what it's like
In her world of therapeutic cupcakes
And visits to the psyche
Her kindly smile is in distress
One thing's clear: She's a mess
While I wait for my next meal
I can comfort her and help her heal
I'm grateful for everything she gives
So I'm going to make sure she lives

VICES VERSUS

She musta had a hard day
Her possessions drop to the table
A constant piled demolished space
She'll not clean even when she's able
I never complain of the constant stress
I have my own BONES of contention
I'm chronically making some kind of mess
That needs her urgent attention
Even though I don't soil my snug domain
I somehow deface hers
A scolding just delays the pain
And mostly makes it worse
But her potpourri of magic tricks
Transforms her stress to tolerance
With those mind-relaxing cocktails mixed
That she visits with such reverence
When her sun sets and her glass is iced
In her world she's so entwined
It never stumped me we're a team
She's got her vices, I've got mine

Table for One

I never had to wipe my kitchen floor
He was always my anteater mop
The fallen counter crumbs never had a chance
Of this he kept on top
A dropped napkin lent retrieval
I would feel an etiquette slip
In my mind there was no upheaval
As he licked the meaty smells from my lip
It never bothered me that the table legs
Lent him a loitering post
To wait in formation in time to beg
For morsels of my roast
I never had a problem with his antics so gauche
And now that he is gone
My heart, my soul misses him so much
It's now just a
Table for One

My Body, My Dog

His head cranes to tilted
But do I feel jilted
That I've just gone naked
In my boudoir?
What does he think
Of skin cheesy and pink
And that I'm no model
From Harper's Bazaar?
Is my vision of manna
In Dolce & Gabbana
The same as his senses
Of sweaty fatigues?
His gaze never changes
As I've gone through my ages
Of fluffy protrusions
In a faulty physique
It seems not to matter
If bod and mind scatter
For he ages 7 times
Faster than me
I can only conclude
I'm a babe to this dude
Who accepts me in reverence
For whatever I'll be

You Can't Get Over Me

We sat in the tuffet and crooned the tube
Always in the groove
The vibes were there
Whatever those were
A TV dinner you often hid
Your diet didn't permit,
But mine did
The movie dates you didn't get
Who cares, you were here, no sweat
You claimed you needed human contact
Wasn't I enough, I don't get the concept
But even so,
Now that I am gone from thee
You're having a hard time
Getting over me
You keep posting on your grievous blog
I'm not your boyfriend,
I'm your DOG.

I Fed Your Dog Tonight

I fed your dog tonight
You were huddling on the street
Music from your soul you couldn't even play
To the Old Town crowd
In their jewel-laden feet
Your dog had no aspiring talent
And neither did you, but still
Life is too short
For canine and man
Not to have crispy fried chicken
At will.
So I ponder sharing a piece of my ATM
Allowance for the day
Knowing I might not subsidize you,
The Rastafarian duo, all the way
When I can't even feed myself
And the guilt I leave behind
Painfully, I must pass you both
With just a buck astray
And hope the next
Soft suckered heart
Will make your day.

New Puppy

There's a new puppy in this chaotic joint
The place where I've been king
Ya' think one's enough
Then things get rough
There's no rest for any living thing
The baby bitch she plays and chews
And bites me on the neck
I thought my energy might wear down
But I like it, what the heck!
Before she came my world was sane
With resting, peace and cuddling
But with her here we run afoul
And end up guiltily huddling
But all for one and one for all
Advantages we see
For I'll never have to howl alone
You alphas, let us be!

SO TOGETHER

Panama hat, shredded straw,
scruffy weathered face
Ambling across the vacant street
At a far-from-marathon pace
He up'd the curb
As did his revering dog
With admiration and grace
A party of two, each to each and this and that
Seeking approval and a welcome pat
They were just "so together"
...Except for the Panama hat

View from a Gucci Bag

Hello world I'm way down here
In my Gucci carry bag
Not getting too excited
Or my tail will surely wag

No room for that
But plenty of space
To see millions of feet
Of the human race

Here comes a chunky working shoe
Of sturdy chewy leather
That shoe could walk me many miles
In any kind of weather

There goes a tall and shiny spike
With long slim legs atop
Her rushing past perfumes the air
And she has no time to stop

I see some tiny dumpling feet
A giggly baby visage
That peeks inside my cozy sack
With a cooing gah-gah message

The feet I know the best of all
Uplift me to the limit
The sack unzips she scoops me out
It's a kibble cuddle minute!

THE DAILY BARK

Out from the rumpled blankets I leap
From my cuddling nest of dreamy sleep
My once limp and resting tail now curled
Says Good Morning to my doggy world
I perch upon the bodies snoozing
Comatose from a night of boozing
My playtime friends are out of sync
Their faces don't wrinkle nor do they blink
An itchy idea jitters through my brain
I'll scratch and vibrate the bed domain
Hoping to reap a rousing reaction
Craving an outing my giant distraction
The dewy grass beckons my first endeavor
That starts my day prepared for whatever
From bedside the ragdoll figures roll
Emerging from vices that take their toll
Those slogging shuffles that hover the floors
Lead gingerly out the patio doors
Though they float around in virtual coma
I'm energized from a bacon aroma
It's ME that ignites the bountiful day
And THEY wouldn't have it any other way

Hard as a Nail

I hate my nails clipped
Don't bring me there
If you try to pull my paw
You'll get nipped
You might even feel stripped
Of your good intentions
Ok, my nails are curled
My flag is unfurled
This is a BONE of contention
You will insist
And I will resist the ordeal
I'm a hard ass with a tail
Soft as mushy oatmeal
Hard as a Nail

Perfect Fit

He's in the gym
She's in the kitchen
They share a common regimen
Amid her daily hustle-bustle
And his reverent quest for muscle
Exhausted as they may be
They make time for ME
Even when they separate in space and time
They Velcro together like rhythm and rhyme
I am the sticky back they peel
Cuddling 'til I want my next meal
I lick my chops and then I savor
More than dog chow is my flavor
They fit together like a hand in a glove
I'm the glue of their sanity and love

$$ Rich vs. Poor $$

I'm poor
I was put out the door
By a wealthy tycoon
On a night of a full glowing moon
I just couldn't adjust
To that life of lush
So here I am

I never knew
How happy I could be
Till I latched onto a part
Of a rusty shopping cart
Here's a good man
Steering his way
Moping around both night and day

And now we're a team
We have no scheme
I'm no longer just a lonely home-bodied bitch

I'm rich

DRUG DOG

I got a cuddly family at home
I love 'em and into their laps I roam
Yeah to them I'm a mushy pushover
But I'm not your usual doggie Rover
I got 2 sides to my persona
My nice guy becomes a loner
I'm a pussy cat
NO don't call me that!
I go to work every day and I love it
Gimme the job I'm not above it
Cuz I'm a drug sniffin' son-of-a-bitch
I don't even have time for an itch
Hiking through people's airport stuff
At the end of the day I've had enough
But my nose takes the urgent cue
I got a damn big job to do
Makin' sure we keep it clean
I'm a snuggly slobbering mighty machine

I Just Want to BE

I once was a playful pup
But today I'm a lazy mutt
I look upon my energized days
Of play and cheer and mischievous ways
Life was good – I had a great time
I warmed your lap and you made me shine
But over the years I began to ache
I love you – make no mistake
I'm sad to say "don't play with me"
In my old age I just want to BE

Just another Walk in the Neighborhood

This is what I hear, bad and good
In my walks through the neighborhood
He's old, He's lazy, He's lanky
Watch out for the yellow house… He's cranky.
They call him Frankenstein
It's just a matter of time….

She's searching for the fountain of youth
Her face lift doesn't tell the truth
The Kosher food delivery is rejected.
She's disconnected.

She's angry and tied to a marriage of battles
He's an unfaithful slacker who tattles.
Their stories don't match all the other gossip.
They should get a grip.
For their information, I don't give a pee
I'm just happy
I'm Me.

Belly Up

They call it being submissive
I call it being cute
When I'm border-line in trouble
Or I don't get snacks to boot
It's my ace in the hole
You could call it a crime
I become in control
When it's BELLY UP time
My soft puppy skin
Is the magnet I need
To win the gal over
It's the call that I heed
So no matter the breach
I'm a pup with a plan
My belly's in reach
So I'll do all I can
It's a matter of fact
When she needs a pickup
I make a doggie impact
When I go BELLY UP

Faith, Hope and Charity

You're strolling by our cage
No matter what your age
We offer you faith
You offer us hope
We're there for you
When you can't cope
With you by our side
They can't put us down
Take us away from
The dog side of town

Puppy UP

He's nestled in the covers
Spread out in peace
The dream of breakfast hovers
And well within reach
A sudden breath of baby air
Arouses me awake
Brushed by soft pink skin and hair
Then I get a little shake
I lift him over my head
Then I cuddle him on my bed
This is not a frolicking child
It's way more wild
And 10 times more fluffy
He's my PUPPY!

I'M WAITING

They left yesterday morning
Can't wait that they return
I know no matter of ticking time
But I've been sitting here for a spin
The doggie sitter she came and gone
And left her Musk perfume
The 90 degree heat puts the kibble she left
To the point of impending doom
But I can feel that a span of time
Has gone without that "cush"
Of a lounging sofa and lagging drool
That I love so much
My meal is not the same with her
As her task is generically immune
I can only hope with slimy anxious tongue
That they return home soon

Pocket Dog

A tiny dog passes by
It's doting owner beaming
She brings it up to heart level
Doggie eyes are gleaming
See how cute he is
Like a photo in a locket
You wear or carry with you
Tucked away in a pocket

Reincarnation

You lacked of sleep at night due to our visage
You tried to keep your heart at a distance
But you saw me, or us, online
Were we real or just benign?
You kissed us 2 dogs Good-bye recently
Falling apart as we departed bluntly
It was not our pledge
To leave you on the ledge
We were taken by the times
You thought we were in our primes
Resisting, your revelations
Were not to renew your doggie-human relations
So soon but you became enthralled
With a needy abandoned puppy who called
FOUL! I was left in an alley
Come take me, I can be all that you rally
Let my body my soul and my color confuse you
I'm the reincarnation of all that amused you
Was it your desperate grieving?
Was it the God of Dogs being deceiving?
You scooped me into your life with a vision
Wondering if you'd made the right decision
I will not let you down
I am reborn from your smile and your frown

A DOG, A SACK, AND A PHONE

I wander the world
In search of whatever
I wouldn't be here
If I was clever
The streets are cold
And so are the folks
I find myself the brunt of jokes
Well I can't help it right now
I always find a way somehow
People think I'm so alone
But I got my dog, my sack and my phone

STAYIN' HOME

The urge to have a change of scene
Has intruded into her routine
I see her trying to get a visa for Brazil
The thought of it makes me ill
She wants an adventure to a distant land
I'll take things that are close at hand
The forms filled out and the papers fly
Anxiety has an endless supply
All that to land in a foreign place
It'd be a doggie waste of time and space
I can only look upon her with pity
While she's dying to leave this familiar city
So as she battles her departure quest
I'll take my cushy smelly nest
How can that excursion be fun at all?
When it even makes MY skin crawl
What good is that, such tasks and stress?
Seems like travel is a mess
Ok I'll be without her for a spree
But staying home sounds good to me

She Shows Me

I am dog with persona strong
But 2 sides rule my wagging
She cuddles me then shows me off
Her "good dog!" keeps her bragging
At home I'm happy on her lap
With play and treats and lickin'
But when were on the road to fame
In overdrive we're kickin'
I've chased around the doggie world
Of poodles, pugs and Collies
Homebound kibbles fit the bill
But so do show-dog follies
We've been to dog shows here and there
At AKC we're Rr-Rr-Revvvvin"
But she's my reward at the end of the day
I've died and gone to Doggie Heaven

Pick Me!!!

The Small Print

I just peed on the floor
Now she put me out the door
Looks like I'm doin' a yard stint
I guess I missed the small print

Got a muzzle full of shoe leather
And I'm out again, in bad weather
Next time can I get a hint?
Looks like I missed the fine print

Just had an unplanned water bowl bath
Oh rats, she's on the warpath
Right now I feel like a piece of lint
For the umpteenth time I've missed the fine print

A Doggie Day

The morning wakes
The blankets rustle
A new day beckons
Gotta hustle
Up from Dreamland
Out to the pee stand
Got the food dished
All that they wished
Hurry, get them in the crates
Close the door in dire straights
Now the doggies make their nest
Cuddled for a long day's rest
Zzzz-Ruff-Zzzz-Ruff
6 o'clock comes they've had enough
Doors fly open, dogs emerge!
A hubbub, bubbub, boisterous SURGE!
The pee-poo cycle starts again
The kitchen lures. The snacks begin
Around the corner gathered and lickin'
Yearning for leftover ham and chicken
When the evening snack is through
Now it's time to pee and poo
While playtime leaves us all aghast
Bedtime comes again at last
Under the covers the dog-moles roam
Woof-Woof Baby, This is Home!

I Hate Rain

I love the feel of tiny drops
Of sprinkling dew and mist
A lazy walk, a path untold
That lets my tongue be kissed
But then the sky breaks open
And so does her umbrella
To the tune of deluge, sharp and wet
Not good for this toasty fella
Let's hurry home, get warm and cozy
Don't take me out here again
I want everything to be comfy and rosy
I HATE RAIN

My Favorite Eats

Apples, scrambled eggs and bacon
Oatmeal cookies, boy I'm aching
Peas and carrots, meatloaf mild
Puffing up this doggie child
Grilled cheese sandwich, chopped banana
Raspberries, blueberries, my kind of manna
Mashed potato, Thanksgiving turkey
Cheez-it crackers, chicken jerky
Tater tots and salmon ends
Given by my doggie friends
Mushroom gravy, leftover noodle
Should I share it with the poodle?
Grilled cheese sandwich, boiled ham
Grab that meat, I'm on the lam!
Beef chunks, rice and other treats
These are a few of my favorite EATS!

DOG-FREE ZONE

My neighbor has a lovely home
Where a bounty of friendly people roam
But I am not the least bit welcome there
He's declared it a dog-free zone

There's parties, food, and lively tunes
But there's nobody captive to tell
How I'm craving the smoky meaty perfumes
In the dog-free zone from hell

There's a baby they coddle 24/7
Kindly as they may be
This does not make the zone a doggie heaven
When they completely exclude me

But at home I have a special accepting place
Where arms are open wide
My loving master with a weathered face
Will keep me by his side

Twenty Minutes

Yesterday this time it was 10 o'clock
Today it's half past 2
Head in my hands I ponder
How much I have to do
Still the few minutes I have
To take break will sneakily slip away
Before I know it spring has past
And here comes Christmas day
As the clock ticks and the kibbles fly
My comfort wafts from this blog
Though life is short I cherish my
20 minutes with my dog

Gypsy

While I wander
People wonder
What I do all day… and night
It's my world, it's not a plight
I have connections, I have tasks
I go and do whatever life asks
At night I guard the homeless in their nests
It's one of my greatest needy tests
By day I watch the school children cross
Sometimes I walk with them, I'm the boss
The dog pound hasn't come for me yet
So for now, I'm nobody's pet
But that's ok, I got wanderlust
For my current world, I just gotta trust
That this is how things were meant to be
For ME

Dear Neighbor

Please pardon my blog
But why do you have a dog?
She is out in your yard both day and night
Perhaps she has an inner plight
She looks and sees my dogs on my terrace
I can almost see her grimace
Please understand, I'm not complaining
Of her occasional barking and whining
I am more concerned that she interact
With loving masters, and that's a fact
I'm just a way-too-caring soul
Call me nosey, if that's your goal
I'll take my lumps but I know what's right
That doggie needs love, through day and night.

2 Gray Hairs

I noticed 2 grey hairs
In the looking glass today
The sign of the times
Will not steal them away
It did lend a reminder
Of the hair of the dog
And the eye of the tiger
And of brushed-off brain fog
That a precious life is short
For my companion, my love
And only determined
By the Dog-God above
Those few sprigs of aging
Will hold me to heart
That one day my lover and I
Will part
So better to savor
And make a vow
To enjoy every gray hair
RIGHT NOW

Double Doggie Grief

I witnessed her decay and decline
A willing participant by moment and day
My heart saw hers outshine
Her crippling submission she tried to downplay
A thankful time throughout the years
My November was no feast
As now I'm in tumultuous tears
My loving black doggie is deceased
I nursed my life back to tolerance
As my next-in-line elder still prancing, resisted
Her concealed well-worn heart
The swollen heart they said she's enlisted
And now I need to prepare for HER demise?
My pain threshold is being heavily tested

She reached her evening's sudden end in a grim shroud
And even as her body hardened
Her heart and soul stayed soft as puffy clouds
I caressed her cooled feet and tail one more time
I prayed that this was the last time I would be pardoned
By the God of Dogs for being such a broken mime.
But so long as one loves dogs
There will be more
Of love and pain
And addictive Doggie lore.

Separation Anxiety

Where am I going?
I feel something tugging
It's not like the hugging
I felt in the past
I hear lots of yelling
In my peaceful dwelling
It's anger I'm smelling
They've caught me aghast
They two were a team
Or was it a dream
Have they run out of steam?
And have I been bypassed?
It looks they're splitting
But would it be fitting
To say they are quitting
When I thought this would last
It wasn't a wedding
Or I'd have been heading
Down the aisle I was dreading
With a ring in my clasp
But this was a paring
There's no doubt of their caring
For it's me they'll be sharing
For their love to outlast

He Doesn't Care

He never noticed my leg veins
Or cared about my body fluff
Although I held the reins
He couldn't get enough
Of the dog walking hiking game
We were a diamond in the rough
I respected him and he did me over again
For all my self-seeing faults
I needn't analyze my jog
Without lipstick doing the waltz
He doesn't judge me – he's my dog.

My Eyes

Before there was he
There was me
There was sun and shadow
Light and dark
Then like magic
I heard his bark
I've always had complete control
But now I have a re-routed goal
I had to make a huge decision
Once I lost my trusty vision
It was hard to release my reluctant disguise
But my service dog has become
MY EYES

I'm Lost

Gate left open for one stinkin' minute
Smelled something great
Had to get in it
Realized I was out of bounds
Ran to the smell off the grounds
Chased my tail and into a spin
Couldn't get back to my yard again
Lost my bearings and went astray
Didn't mean to run away
I'm LOST
She'll miss me and be frantic
The whole house'll be in a panic
I don't know how to get back
So best just to move forward in my tracks
And hope my absence won't cause too much pain
Cuz I just can't find my way home again
I'm LOST

I am a High Desert Dog

I am FOX the puppy.
Coyote is my kin.
A high desert dog he is.
And so my quest begins.

My eyes are sparkling, expressive,
Magical and GOLD
So as I question "What am I?"
Let my "tail" unfold.

A sunny day, a kindly soul,
A cuddling human friend
Discovered me, a shining star
My heart was on the mend.

I came to live with them that day,
A shy and hungry pup.
A brand new home, a hopeful life,
Before my time was up.

It wasn't easy when I arrived.
I had a mind of my own.
I wanted to be king of the pack,
And not to be alone.

But I was the new guy in the house.
I had to wait my turn.
My doggie family must adjust,
With many things to learn.

For it's never easy for anyone
To fit into a pack.
It takes time for all to understand
What you possess and lack.

My shelter roots did bring me here,
But a special bond I feel.
The desert breeze, the wanderlust,
The search for my next meal.

For what the future holds for me,
My mind is in a fog.
I'll do my part, but in my heart,
I am a High Desert Dog

FIRST CHRISTMAS

Short-term memory
Dogs have they say
But I don't see it quite that way

I know of times
Of yelping and yip
It certainly was an awesome trip

Got doggie snacks
Just for not messing
What a delicious kindly blessing

For now I don't see
The festive hanging things
Or how they would bring bling bling bling

Different than before
Pretty quiet here
Where treats would magically appear

Can't help dwelling on the past
I hope this feeling won't last
This is my first Christmas
Without him

The Measure of a Smile

The vibe came from a soft hand above
Before the stroke of luck and love
You flipped over to get the feel
Of a belly massage from top to heel
I notice a gleaming toothy smile
Saying you want to stay a while
You lie in complete ecstasy
Wondering what more you'll get from me
But when I see your lips spread wide
To the maximum teeth-y side
I can see the smiling wisdom teeth
This is maximum doggie peace

The Farewell Dog

I met the dog in my daily task
Picking up the mail in my driving mask
He sat in Sphynx-like allure
On my neighbors grass
Guiding me through my tour
He caused an impasse
With his most kindly focused eyes
The staring contest that rendered me paralyzed
Through my community
That offered no immunity
From the pooling blue eyes
Of the Farewell Dog

I, DOG, WILL NEVER LEAVE

You needed me on a lonely day
A friend, a lover passed away
I came along to help you grieve
I, Dog, Will Never Leave

A bad day came, a world of stress
You had no one to address
You looked to faith, I helped you believe
I, Dog, Will Never Leave

Your body and your mind fell ill
Over time you lost your will
You thought there would be no reprieve
I, Dog, Will Never Leave

Your cherished pet, I'm the one you found
Adopted, nurtured, shared common ground
I love you too, now for me you bereave
I, Dog, Will Never Leave

Not Too Late

I've not much time left
But I feel so alone
Even with my loving family nearby
I'm missing that big bad BONE.
People tell me I'll be fine
But I'm not gonna hear it
I'm a wise old ass
And I don't need to fear it
I'm gonna put the drizzle
On the zhizel
And get me a friend
Who can help me see my way ahead
To the very end
I'll just love him and lay like a log
Cuz it's never too late to get a dog.

www.ingramcontent.com/pod-product-compliance
Lightning Source LLC
LaVergne TN
LVHW020134080526
838202LV00047B/3939